T5-BQA-924

THE LAST REPATRIATE

A NOVELLA BY MATTHEW SALESSES

Mary & Jaime,

You guys are awesome and this bookstore is awesome. Keep raising that baby to kick ass!

NOUVELLA

2011

THE LAST REPATRIATE

A Nouvella book / published 2011

Design by Daniel D'Arcy
Cover photo by Mick Waller

For information go to:
nouvellabooks.com

Printed in the United States of America.

First Edition.

For my two girls,
Grace and Cathreen

11 *of 500*

The Last Repatriate

I

IMAGINE THE THICK FOREST of Korea, late autumn, 1950, sunset, the sentimental angle of light through the pines. Here, a boy of nineteen sits on a mossy log, reading a letter from his sweetheart in Virginia. He hasn't had one from her in weeks.

Dear Ted,

Thanks for your letters. I guess you weren't ready for war, as I reckoned you wouldn't be. I warned you, remember? I should have told you then that I wasn't ready either. I cannot stand the distance.

Can you form a picture of their relationship, young love, the expectation of marriage, the time period, the idealistic kid Theodore Dickerson must have been to march off to war and leave his fiancée behind? He flicks an ant off the letter and rubs his floppy ears. He sits at the edge of a bivouac, where other soldiers, his peers we might say, finish their lunch. They disapprove of him, the still-emotional boy who can cry over words in a land of flourishing death. Theodore, known as Teddy in Virginia, Teddy Bear in Korea, a corporal in the United States Army, reads the last paragraph, back stiff, hands gripping the paper; his face gives out like a torn spider web. He hurries into the trees, in his head a vision of Beth twirling a white dress around her ankles. He weaves deeper, ignoring orders to stop, and collapses in a small clearing.

I reckon I'm not strong enough. Neither of us is. I know this will hurt you—even about the war you were a romantic—but I've started going with George Watson. He doesn't need to prove himself. I left the ring with your mother.

I will always love you.

Beth

Teddy lies back, a memory snaking up in him: he and George damming the stream behind Beth's house, as kids, the three of them taking turns doing the dead man's float. He draws his pistol and holds the steel to his temple as the sky bruises into dusk.

A noise, a low voice, frightens him to his feet. He points his gun ahead of him and turns in a slow circle. His palms sweat. He switches his gun to his left hand, wipes his right on his shirt, and is about to switch back when a rifle butt clubs the base of his neck.

IMAGINE WINTER at the doorstep of Manchuria, Teddy with a black eye, bones like poles in a kite of skin. The POW camp is a wide stretch of land with a river guarding three sides, mountains beyond, barbed wire around the fourth, one small mud hut for every hundred prisoners. Teddy touches the ground near the fence. Frozen. Two guards in parkas talk farther off. The prisoners have only the clothing they wore when captured in the fall, in the southern country. Teddy tests the dirt. Then he finds it: a spot soft enough to dig. He slips the letter out from inside his pants and buries it, glancing back, shaking.

For the first month, no one spoke to him, no more than a command to get out of the way or to help bury dead. At night the prisoners sleep side by side, so close they can't turn over—this warmth is his only contact; it is the warmth keeping them alive. When it is time for their one meal, they stumble to the frozen river, which they use as a toilet, and clear enough ice to break a hole through. There, they fill a pot for soup. Sometimes Teddy smacks his lips in his sleep, waking the man next to him, in his dreams a clear glass of water.

His only friend is a man called Red, whom the others say is the last prisoner dumb enough to fight back. "Red versus the Reds," they say. Red is from Virginia, too. Teddy tells him about the circle of soft earth. Another prisoner, O'Neil, breaks in.

"Corporal Teddy Dickerson," Teddy says, saluting.

"You know rank don't matter here," O'Neil says. "They call you Teddy Bear?"

Two guards drag a naked POW into the snow and dump a bucket of water on him.

"A tunnel," O'Neil is saying. Teddy turns away.

"Don't worry about those screaming skulls," Red says as the naked man heaves.

AT NIGHT, TEDDY FEELS the back of the man next to him rising and falling with breath. The man's elbow jabs his side. A stink rises when his arm moves. The Chinese have arrived in the camp and have been sewing chicken gizzards into the armpits of the sick. Some prisoners talk about eating the gizzards.

THERE IS ONE PRISONER, Tiny, of course huge, who predicts when others will die. He pushes Teddy at dinner. Teddy doesn't understand. Tiny dips a dirty hand into Teddy's soup, just cabbage and water. "You got two weeks, maybe."

Teddy stares past to where Beth's letter is buried. Then Red is there.

Teddy watches the rock smash Red's ear, notices the frostbite for the first time. The ear seems to crack like ceramic. Red lands a good shot on Tiny's chin, but then he's in a choke hold, his eyes blinking, red trickling down into his red beard.

Teddy can't help himself; he slurps down the rest of his soup.

WE SEE TEDDY HESITATING over a frozen body. Finally he tears a strip from the uniform, and another, then ties the two strips into a band around Red's ear. At night, he sleeps next to Red, smelling the iron from Red's blood. His teeth chatter. He doesn't know how to stop. His fingers dip between ribs when he scratches himself. He taps the bones like a piano he hears inside of him.

TEDDY AND RED AND O'NEIL rip up uniforms before burials, huddle behind the huts, glue the cloth together with mashed-up rice and water. It's hard for

Teddy to save his rice, counting down the fortnight Tiny gave him. His ribs sting as if something is stuck between them, though nothing is there, then pulse in and out like a busted light. Red says they'll use the cloth to wave down the Air Force.

After two days, O'Neil's fingers turn blue. We see them rubbing each other's hands. Teddy stops when a cry carries across the grounds. He remembers a day in Cracker's Neck when a donkey split its hoof on a buried hunk of metal; it writhed there for an hour before the owner came and shot it. For some reason now, Teddy starts sobbing. O'Neil shakes his head. Red stares at them, then takes off at a sprint.

When the noises stop, Red reappears with another man over his shoulder. He runs into one of the huts at the far edge of the camp.

IN THE MORNING, O'Neil pulls Teddy out of his hut. Teddy stumbles, stepping on a sick prisoner. Outside, everyone is gathered. "They're taking him to the Hole," they whisper. The guards shove Red out of a hut fifty feet away. They've beaten him, his skin a map of lakes and mountains. Blood shines on his face in the early light.

"What's the Hole?" Teddy asks. No one answers.

Red tries to smile, his mouth swollen. His eyelids are crusted shut. One of the guards punches his kidneys. He spits up blood, more blood, all over himself. When he falls, the guards kick him until he keeps going. O'Neil runs his hand over his head and whispers, "Red versus the Reds."

AT NIGHT, TEDDY DREAMS he is gutting Red's armpit like a fish. Then he slips the gizzard inside. In his dream, he knows what the Hole is. When he wakes, he lies in the dark trying not to cry on the man next to him. Finally, he can't take it anymore. He gets up, ignoring the swears. Outside, he digs Beth's letter back up, feels the thick paper between his fingers.

NOW WE SEE FIVE SHAPES running over the hills beyond the camp in the rain, sparse trees, miles of bush and land and no real destination, the old uniforms' cloth like the train of a gown. Teddy and O'Neil and three others. They stop once the rain stops, and pass food around, their clothes soaked, eating in gulps. But as they're packing back up, they see two shadows on the hills.

"We could kill them," Teddy says suddenly. "Hide behind these here trees and get them before they know what happened. I'm telling you, we could."

They crouch down close to the ground. "What if there's more?" one of them asks.

"The rain covered our tracks," O'Neil says. "But it makes theirs clear as day. They'll be followed if they don't come back."

"I have two little boys at home."

They argue for minute; then the smallest of them, the cook who helped with supplies, stands. The guards are closer now. They see the movement. "Shit," O'Neil says. The cook has a good lead. Teddy starts after him, but O'Neil grabs his arm. The others put up their hands.

Soon the guards reach them, panting, and the first holds his pistol on them as the second follows the cook, stops, and fires. Teddy turns to see him walk over and knife the cook in the neck, knife him again, and again, and return calmly.

BACK AT THE CAMP, they're held in a sort of schoolhouse with mud-covered windows, one of them tied by his biceps to the roof; his arms turn as pale as the snow. Teddy is lashed to a post and forced to watch O'Neil beaten. A Chinese colonel with a doughy face digs his fingernails into Teddy's eyes to keep them open.

After O'Neil passes out, they lead Teddy, like Red, to the Hole: a cement vault neither long enough to lie in or high enough to sit in, off separate from the huts. They seal him in with a wooden pallet and roll a boulder on top so it's completely dark.

The first thing he does is vomit. Before they shoved him in, he noticed the layer of shit on the bottom. He can smell other people's vomit, too. He managed not to break his fall with his hands, but he can feel the slime on his bruised knees. He lifts his fingers to his mouth, sucks the blood and sweat.

Two days later, his tongue is swollen and rubbery. His fingers tap his shaking legs. One-two-three-four. "Red, are you there?" He presses Beth's letter to his nose, trying to smell something farther away, in Virginia, muttering: "Beth. Beth. Beth. Beth."

AFTER THREE DAYS in the Hole, he is moved back to the schoolhouse. This time, the guards hit him carefully and then feed him. They give him pork, maggoty fish, even garlic—he doesn't know where this food has come from. A pistol cracks his ribs. When he can no longer take it, he blacks out.

They wake him, give him a little water, something that looks like bacon, beat him again. Still, he almost thanks them for the food. He almost thanks the Chinese colonel for pushing a document in front of him, something to sign.

THE COLONEL SETS UP a school of Communism, at first thirty sitting and listening, then fifty scribbling invented confessions, then a hundred speaking into a recorder, waiting for their reward of eggs and rice. Teddy sees O'Neil outside the schoolhouse on the first morning. Before a guard appears, O'Neil punches Teddy in the gut.

On Teddy's tape recording, you can hear him give his name and say he's always wanted to be on the radio. "Are folks back home listening to this?" he asks, "I reckon I've started to understand things."

Outside the schoolhouse, a man hangs on a peg by his skin.

IN 1953, the war ends. The POWs transfer to a neutral site in a UN compound, guarded by Indian custodial forces. Along the neutral zone, a US Army jeep drives back and forth, blaring a message from its loudspeakers: "We have reason to believe some of you are being forcibly prevented from returning. We have taken steps to assure your safety. The Indian guards will receive any of you who desire to come home."

We see Teddy in a room like a visiting room of a prison, the Chinese colonel telling him not to believe the Army. He says Teddy cannot go home. He is one of them, a Progressive. He and twenty-two others have said they will not repatriate to America; they will go to China. He is lucky, the colonel says, to have been chosen.

Teddy massages his temples, taps his fingers on his head. He remembers, on the hike to the POW camp from

Pyongyang, a man dipped his face into a bag he'd been ordered to haul, hungry enough to eat anything. Later, he fell back screaming and holding his stomach. A guard passed the bag on. Inside was a chewed block of TNT.

Teddy feels a hand on his shoulder. With all the weight he's lost, his ears look huge. He has wrinkles around his soft eyes. Outside, the Army blasts its message again. When he tried to talk options with the others, telling them about his family in Virginia, one of them said, "Teddy Bear, you're one of us."

NIGHT NOW, everyone asleep in their bunks. Teddy pushes off his blanket; underneath, he is fully dressed. For a moment, he stares around at the others with their cold sheets drawn close like arms—all of these men have families waiting. His fingers go to the letter in his pocket. He sneaks past them and hurries across the compound to the gate, glancing over his shoulder. An Indian sentry guards the entrance.

"I reckon I got a toothache," Teddy says, cupping his mouth.

He looks back at the gray building. He isn't one of them.

FROM THE COMPOUND, the Army flies Teddy to Tokyo. A military doctor gives him a full exam. In the Army hospital, a photographer looks through his view-finder: Teddy and two nurses, one on each arm, the doctor waiting to the side. A few minutes earlier, Teddy watched his knees and elbows fold, almost flinching at the rubber reflex hammer. Now he rubs his joints self-consciously as his eyes follow the girls out of the room.

"You're quite the hero," the doctor says.

"Am I?"

"You know that picture's going to be in the newspaper. Your family will be happy to see you." The doctor touches his head. "How're the sessions going? The shrink?"

"I reckon he's mostly interested in what happened in the camp."

"What did happen?"

No answer. The smell of disinfectant rises from the hall.

"You got anyone waiting on you?"

Teddy leans forward. He shakes his head, more to clear his mind than to say no.

The doctor smiles.

"What?" Teddy asks.

"You're all set."

A nurse accompanies him back to the hotel, her arm beneath his shoulder blades.

TEDDY HAS A ROOM at the Dai Iti, a nice place, not too expensive, but overwhelming after the camp. Running water, room service. We can tell his thoughts are on home as he sits lotus-style on the bed. Two Army investigators stand in front of him. They wear civilian clothing. The first—Cumby, a silk shirt, a smooth talker—leans against the dresser. The second—Cole, an old suit, an old hand—stands by a mirror. Teddy's had a haircut, a slight wave across his forehead. He catches himself in the mirror as he sets the alarm on the clock radio, a strange thing to him, time.

"Doctor says I'm a hero."

"That's what we've been telling you," Cumby says. "You seeing it now? How'd you like them Army nurses?" A look passes between the investigators. "I'd guess you haven't seen a woman in three years. What do you say we get out of here? Go for a drive, maybe. Show you the city. You'll love Tokyo. Beautiful city. Beautiful girls."

Cole pretends to consider the idea.

"Lights everywhere, like the whole city is floating on lights."

"I reckon I'd like to see it," Teddy says, looking into the mirror again.

Cole slips some papers into his briefcase. "A hero should have the right."

THEY TAKE HIM to a hostess club, the *Lov Bar*, once trendy. Private booths surround an open area in the center where women mill around the bar—at these places, a hostess will join a group for a fee, sometimes go beyond. They sit in a closed-off booth, with neon receded lights, a half-empty bottle of whiskey and the briefcase on the table. Cole refills Teddy's glass.

"We're just doing our job, Teddy," Cumby says. "The Army's got need of this kind of intelligence. You'd be doing us a real help. Saving lives. Saving people like you."

Teddy squints, presses the heels of his hands against his eyes.

"You okay?"

"I reckon I don't remember everything."

"I envy your position, you know? Everything you survived—the girls'll love your story. The press already loves it."

Cole opens the door to their booth.

"I'm fine," Teddy says, taking another sip of whiskey.

"The fresh air will do you good."

"I done some things I'm not proud of."

Cole looks toward the bar and nods. A pop song trills over the speakers as the whiskey burns in Teddy's throat. Soon a hostess slides in beside him, a short woman who gives the impression of a long body. "How-are-you?" she says in a thick accent. She touches his arm.

"You're meeting a real American hero tonight," Cumby says. "Killed a hundred Koreans with his bare hands."

Teddy runs his fingers through his hair. He is stunned by the girl's beauty, his sudden inability to swallow. He nods.

"Boy survived everything the Reds threw at him. Ain't that right, Teddy? Ain't that right?"

"I don't know," Teddy says. The hostess stretches out her long neck, as if on cue. Teddy has never lost himself in a neck before. "Yeah, everything." She slides closer.

"Made you write things for them, say things? Just like the other boys?"

At once, Teddy remembers the cold of a gun to his head. He's drunk enough to think the girl understands everything. "Other boys? I'm the first one back of the ones they made stay. I reckon I went through more than any of them *other boys*."

"I don't know," Cumby says. "What you told us ain't nothing new."

Cole refills Teddy's glass.

"They beat me," Teddy says, slurring, shaking. "They brainwashed me."

The hostess looks up, expectant. Cumby and Cole wait.

"I almost escaped," Teddy says. "Almost got a whole group of us out of there. Red got killed. They stuck me underground. They made me do things, sure. The bastards. I led the Progressives, all of us acting Commie enough just to stay safe, not get beat. I had to lead them. I basically hung a man on a hook for making trouble. Could have been my own hands." He drums the table, looks into the hostess's face, snaps back. "I tell you I did anything to survive, worse than you'd reckon possible."

Cole writes steadily, the briefcase open for some time, the papers on the table. Cumby glances over in apprehension, remembering the rumors of courts-martial. Teddy talks and drinks and talks on.

LATER, BACK IN THE DAI ITI, we see yen wrapped in a pair of stockings, clothing on the floor, the hostess on top of Teddy, looking down.

He says: "I have to tell you something."

She stares back, smiling blankly.

"This is my first time."

TEDDY MAKES A TRIUMPHANT RETURN, written up in the newspapers and welcomed with a parade. We see him in a gazebo, brushing off his uniform beside the town's white-teethed mayor, the mountains of Virginia behind him, the local high school band attempting the national anthem.

"He took everything the Commies threw at him and survived. Now he's finally returned to us, the prodigal son, the pride of Virginia. He has made our town proud. Why don't you say a few words, Theodore?"

Teddy steps forward, slapped on the back. He sees his parents in the front of the crowd, his mother stooped over from years of stress and his father staring intently; he looks past his neighbors and friends. When he spots

Beth, a smile forms. Then he notices George beside her, and his face falls. We see a girl, Kate, he doesn't yet recognize, standing in the first row, a short, vibrant girl, dark brown hair, sea-shifting eyes, nearly black freckles like holes in her cheeks a bird pecked to get inside her mouth.

"It's good to be home, I reckon. In the camp, I didn't know what to think. I thought of Cracker's Neck so many times—I needed that piece of home. I did things I had to. I tried to get back. I got past them Reds, trying to get past them Reds, to escape."

The mayor cuts him off. "The pride of Virginia." A drum roll starts and shouts rise from the crowd. The band plays again, "Dixie" this time. Teddy looks for Beth, but she's gone.

THE DICKERSON HOME is a small, country affair, clapboards, wooden furniture, etc., in the kitchen an old dining table with oak chairs carved by a great-grandfather who died in the Civil War. His mom hugs him hard. His pop stands behind them, near the sink, the same wave to his thinning hair, the same floppy ears.

"Did you see how they loved you?" his mom asks.

"I'm a hero now, Momma."

His pop shakes his hand like a stranger. "Always said you'd be someone someday, son. Always said so, didn't I?"

Teddy steps away from his mom, sits down at the kitchen table, feeling old. He reaches his hands around his head, starting on his forehead and moving to the back where his fingers weave around his brain. He grimaces—a headache stirring.

LATER THAT NIGHT, he lies in his childhood bed, a wet facecloth resting above his eyes, the lids open, unblinking. On the nightstand is the engagement ring Beth returned to his mom while he was at war.

He is in the middle of a flashback. He seems surrounded by darkness; then he understands that he is in the Hole, the smell seeping into his nose. "Beth," he whispers. "Beth."

We see his mom rushing into the room. She finds him thrashing on his bed, his arms and legs uncontrollable, his body shaking, his mouth foaming slightly.

"Frank," his mom shouts.

His pop runs in and they hold him down together.

"Teddy, look at me. Look at me, baby. Your momma's right here. Please, wake up. Please."

IN THE MORNING, Teddy walks into the kitchen as his mom cooks breakfast, the scent of bacon drawing him toward his first Southern meal in three years. When she turns to him, red-eyed, he asks her what the matter is. She looks back, not moving, as if he's forgotten her, as if he doesn't know who she is, and he feels confused, a coldness running up his arms.

HE GOES FOR A WALK after lunch, down their typical small-town street: kids loitering, a few shops along the sides, a convenience store, a liquor store, a drug store, etc. As he passes a group of high school girls, they call out to him. They wave and smile, recognizing him from the parade. He hurries past, turns down a side street, and runs as if they are chasing him.

He dips inside the drug store, the same one where he used to go as a boy, for cherry sodas. A familiar girl browses the candy aisle, carrying a bag of root beer candies, which she shuttles now and then between her lips.

He stares, tries to turn without losing sight of her; at last, he recognizes her freckles. Kate. "You used to chew them candies the same way when you was a kid," he says.

She doesn't look up. "You used to make fun of me with that Watson boy."

He flinches.

"I saw you yesterday," she says.

"Reckon everyone in town saw me."

"Guess you already let it go to your head." She fingers a pack of gum, places it back on the shelf.

"They say I'm a hero."

"Who's they?"

"I don't know. The mayor."

A strand of brown hair loosens from behind her ear. "Just stomping for votes," she says. Finally, she glances up. "You're wounded, I reckon."

He reaches for his face, rubs his left shoulder where a guard once dragged a cigar for fun, pulls his earlobe where the colonel touched a hot gun barrel.

"Inside, I mean. I can tell."

"How can you tell?"

She smiles. "Heard you and Beth didn't work out."

His hands drop to his sides and he stiffens.

"I see her around, sometimes," she says. "With your friend, George. The three of you used to be so stupid and mean."

"I'm different now," he says. "A whole other person."

As she stares, he draws himself up, vulnerable and honest.

"Maybe it all done you good."

"Let me buy them candies for you," he says.

Her freckles burn. "Ain't no way. My daddy sees me eating these, he'll beat me."

"Reckon he won't be mad if I got them for you," he says. "You seen how things is different for me now."

AT DINNER, chicken-fried steak and corn cobs, his pop smiling grimly, his mom staring at Teddy's plate, unable to concentrate, Teddy says, "I ran into Kate today."

"Who's that one?" his pop asks, chomping a row of corn.

"The Laney girl, Frank." His mom coughs. "Her momma killed herself?"

Teddy had forgotten that.

"Son, you can choose any girl you want."

"I ain't said nothing about choosing, Pop."

His mom spears her steak with her fork. "You and that Watson boy used to pull her hair. You'd come home talking about how she done you wrong, even when you was six years old."

Teddy squeezes his temples, pinches his eyes shut.

"Oh, I'm sorry, baby." His mom laughs nervously.

He opens and closes his eyes.

"Teddy?"

The room seems to darken; the walls shrink. He reaches into his pocket. He seems to hear his own voice say, "Beth, Beth, Beth, Beth."

"Teddy?"

The room closes in on him, and goes black.

When he wakes, it's morning, the sun crowning the horizon, voices slipping through the cracked door. His clothes are neatly folded and laid out at the end of his bed. He dresses, listening.

"But what's happening to him? He's different. He's not my Teddy. He's not."

"Just stop it. I reckon you're driving me crazy."

"Momma?" Teddy asks, pulling on his jeans, sizes bigger than he remembers.

THAT AFTERNOON, he takes another walk to clear his head, in the woods this time. We see him stepping through the cool shadows with his hands dug deep in his pockets, talking to himself. He's trying not to think about Korea. As his arm brushes a birch tree, he hears singing, a voice cresting on invisible waves.

Old Missus married 'Will the Weaver'.
Willum was a gay deceiver.
Look away! Look away! Look away!
Dixie Land.

Near the edge of the woods, he spots Kate kneeling in the moss picking flowers. Daisies. She sings on, not noticing him, daisies in her hair.

Old Missus acted the foolish part
And died for a man that broke her heart.
Look away! Look away! Look away!
Dixie Land.

He watches from behind the tree. When he continues on, he picks up the tune, whistling it, making his way down through the woods. His hair blows crooked in the wind. Finally, he reaches a brook. Across the water, a large manor-like house stands on a well-tended lawn. Beth's house. We hear him crumpling something in his pocket. He stops whistling, turns away.

IF WE FOLLOW KATE HOME to the run-down cottage she shares with her daddy, which looks like an old farmhouse without farmland, on her porch the next morning, beside a weather-beaten rocking chair, sits a bucket of daisies. Her daddy, a middle-aged, cruel-featured man who misses his dead wife, steps out onto the porch to the reflection of light off of the tin. He stops. He opens the door again, yells for his daughter.

He settles into the rocking chair as Kate pounds downstairs.

We see her emerge, roughly dressed, her hair morning-mussed, sleep in her eyes, yet gorgeous, of course, for this is our girl to fall in love with. She looks at her daddy with a cautious worship.

"These for you?" he asks, rocking.

"I don't know."

"They sure ain't for me."
She hesitates. Her daddy's eyes narrow. Then she rushes toward the flowers; as she picks up the bucket, he kicks out, almost hitting her.

TEDDY QUICKLY BUSIES HIMSELF with love. Imagine the Fifties and an ex-POW given three months off (with back pay), knowing the experience of sudden deaths, nursing a broken heart. He leaves daisies on her porch each morning before she wakes; he talks with her daddy; he consults the town pastor; he lines daisies along the sides of the church pews; he buys a new car; he writes her an anonymous letter.

When Kate shows up at the church, at the letter's request, an old but well cared-for building, the daisies seem to tint everything yellow. No one seems inside—then Teddy pops up with a bouquet.

"You can't do this," she whispers, both surprised and unsurprised.

"I'm in love with you, Kate. We're going to be married." He places the bouquet in her arms.

"No, we ain't."

"I asked for your hand."

"Just because my daddy says yes don't mean I got to."

But then Teddy kneels and brings out a jewelry box. We see it's the ring he gave Beth, the ring from the bedside table. Kate's lip trembles. She's never been given jewelry before.

"I know it's not much," Teddy says. "It's just until we get married. I promise the wedding ring'll be nicer."

She can't stop herself. She takes the box.

She stares down at the ring. It seems familiar, but she can't place it. She wants it. She holds her breath inside her until it struggles to get out. But at last, she says: "I don't even know you." She pushes the ring away, and runs out before she can change her mind, her dark hair swishing around her neck.

WE FOLLOW HER HOME AGAIN. Her daddy in the rocking chair on the porch as usual, chewing tobacco. He spits into a rusted spittoon, a wrinkled T between his eyebrows.

"I can't marry him," Kate says. "He ain't never even been nice to me before."

"Nice don't mean nothing. He's a hero. Your momma—"

"This ain't about Momma."

"You better watch what you say."

She tears up, sniffling. "This ain't about Momma, Daddy."

He rocks back, his gaze falling into the distance. "I said to watch it."

IN THE CHURCH REFECTORY, Kate readies herself to walk down the aisle. A space has been set aside for her dressing room. White ribbons and too many decorations cover the walls. She twirls before a tall mirror, majestic in her wedding dress, her skin porcelain, her blue eyes dazed and wet, staring at her reflection. Her mother seems to appear behind her, a somber freckled woman of similar features.

Kate takes a long look. She twirls and twirls.

When she gets out into the main part of the church, she sees everything Teddy has prepared. Everyone in town has come, the mayor in the front pew beside Teddy's parents.

Teddy stands at the altar waiting for her, looking—as we alone can tell—toward Beth in the far back of the church, then shifting his gaze to Kate when the wedding march begins. Everyone stands. Kate advances down the aisle. Teddy stares into the crowd once more before turning back to be married. His fingers shake.

Kate smiles sadly through the veil, eyes her father, takes Teddy's arm.

AFTER THE CEREMONY, at Teddy's house for their wedding night, his parents away, they stand in his bedroom, he still in his tux, her in her dress. She sighs, and he sits down on the bed.

"I wish I'd known when we was young that I was going to marry you," he says.

"Why?"

"I could have loved you all along."

"You don't love me," Kate says.

"Why else do you reckon I'd marry you." He lies back.

"I wish you hadn't," she says. "What are you going to do if we have us a baby. You ain't going to be around for it."

"I could quit the Army," Teddy says, smoothing a wrinkle on the sheets.

"You're a hero, Teddy. You need the Army. I reckon the Army needs you."

"I had to marry you fast before these three months end," he says, "because I couldn't let anyone else have you."

We see her soften. They both make up their minds at once. Teddy moves toward her. She retreats.

"I can't do that."

"Not tonight?"

"I just—" She holds her hands up, palms out, and plops down beside him. "Can we just sleep here? I reckon I can't go home."

She curls up on his single bed, in her gown. He circles around to the other side and lies beside her, not touching her. They lie like that for a while, still dressed, the room darkening.

Later, he says, "Kate. I ain't trying to force you to marry me. I reckon I should have asked you first."

She's silent.

"Seeing you—I don't know. You looked like everything I needed."

THE FIRST DAY OF THEIR HONEYMOON, they drive into the countryside in the new Studebaker, the mountains rising in front of them. They park in a lot for the Daniel Boone Wilderness Trail and hike up toward Boone cabin for a picnic. After an hour, they reach a rest area with metal tables, but Kate keeps walking. They lay his mom's blanket in some dandelions farther on, each taking two corners. They open the picnic basket to their sandwiches, sloppily made that morning—he the ham, she the cheese—and she starts to cry.

"I don't know what we're doing," she says. "I used to dream of getting married—" She can't go on.

We see Teddy's surprise, as if this complaint has come out of nowhere. He runs a finger along the line of his chin. "You look beautiful today," he says.

She doesn't stop crying.

He shifts over on the blanket. He sweeps an arm around her, but when he feels her trembling, he drops it. His hand dips into his pocket, withdraws again. "You know, I thought of you in the war."

She turns her head to him, teary. His heartbeat quickens.

"When I was locked up in the camp."

"You did?"

"I tried to escape," he says. "Me and four others. They shot one of us."

"And you thought of me then?"

He bites the insides of his cheeks. "I reckon so. Just a flash of your face. I wanted to come home so bad."

"And then what happened?"

"And then we went back to the camp, that's all."

"You didn't fight back?"
The wind blows her hair into her face, and he reaches for his own face, brushing the edge of his mouth in

the same spot her hair fell on hers. Something tries to burrow out of him as she sniffles. Then he stands and raises his arms as if holding a rifle.

"I had me this friend, Red. When we see them China-men coming up over the hill, he just starts running. We follow him. Then they're shooting at us. Bam. Bam. Red goes down. Hits him right in the neck. 'Keep running,' Red says. 'Keep running.' But they're on us. We ain't got a chance."

He collapses onto the blanket, takes a big bite of his sandwich as if to eat the lie. He gulps water, lies back and stares at the clouds.

Kate watches him, no longer crying. She scoots toward him. Then she lies beside him, brings her head to his shoulder.

Later, he repacks the picnic basket and she folds the blanket. She holds it in her arms like a baby, her blue eyes shining down. When she sees Teddy looking at her, her lips purse, confused.

Teddy hears a branch snap. He comes to attention, reaches for where he would carry his gun. The wind rustles through the reeds and a bird flies up overhead. He glances nervously at Kate. She cradles the blanket and smiles. "Remember, when I was nine," she says, "you carried me all the way home from the drug store after I sprained my ankle?"

He eyes the woods, slings the basket over his shoulder. He lifts her in his arms and runs back over the trail to the Studebaker.

In the motel, they lie in the same positions as in his bedroom, still not touching, both on their sides, he turned toward her, she away. She lies awake, thoughtful. After a while, she rolls over and faces him. His eyes open, startling her. He wasn't asleep, either. They stare at each other. We watch her neck stretch as she kisses him on the forehead.

The next day, they drive to Claytor Lake. They climb up the hill to the cliff that sticks out over the water, from which kids used to dive in the summer. In the morning, she said she wanted to remember that. In the lake is a reflection of the sky and the trees and the sun. A flock of geese flies overhead in a U shape. It's a warm November afternoon, but still only about fifty degrees. Teddy stares at her thighs shifting in her jeans as they make their way up, around them the rustling of birds he and his pop used to hunt.

At the top, she stands near the edge of the cliff in a light jacket, facing him with her back to the lake. A smile crosses her mouth, dilating freckles. Then she takes a step backward, as if to dare him, and cocks her head like a puppy.

What does she want? He holds out his arms, approaching slowly. She backs away again. One more step and she'll fall.

He stops and says, "Crazy's crazy."

Suddenly, her face drops. She stares back as if he's slapped her, her eyes seeming to rattle in their sockets. "George used to say that, right?" she says, snapping her fingers. "Like mother like daughter."

The words had come to him automatically. "I'm sorry," he says, hating George even more. She looks about to cry. But instead, she turns, jumps into the air, and is gone.

He panics. He steps closer to the edge, watches the splash. Then he backs up to get room to run. His breath seems to catch in the air, like a goose shot out of the sky, and he dives in after her.

In the lake, she gasps for breath. The cold cripples her lungs. The cold makes ice of their clothes. The cold seems to stab through his pores, but his body remembers those three winters in North Korea. She struggles, splashing. She grabs her chest and sinks. He strokes out over the lake. "Kate," he calls. "Kate." When he reaches her, he wraps an arm around her ribs. Water pours into his mouth. He sputters.

At first, they don't seem to go anywhere. He kicks and they dip underwater. He brings them back up by will. The lake stretches out before them, endless. His bones seem to vibrate. His legs want to go numb, feel nothing. But he wills them in to shore.

He pushes her onto the cold ground, her hair roped around him, and she lies on her back, shivering and hugging herself. He crawls up next to her, catching his breath. As soon as he can, he runs to the Studebaker for the picnic blanket. He resists the urge to cover himself with it as he returns. He pulls off her clothes and wraps the blanket around her. She's able to get to her feet, and they stumble to the car, at last.

He turns on the heat, strips off his shirt, kicks off his shoes and socks. She wraps the blanket around them both and they huddle close for warmth.

"Thank you," she mouths, her lips purple and small.

BY THE TIME HE DRIVES BACK to his house, she's caught ill. That night, she lies in his bed, the color drained from her face. She mumbles strings of nonsense. He sits beside her. We see his mom entering, checking Kate's temperature, leaving. We hear Kate breathing words, "Please, don't," to no one in particular.

Teddy leans in, trying to hear her. He holds her hand, plays with her ring. She's still wearing Beth's engagement ring, below the wedding band. He stops.

As Kate falls sicker, not coming out of it, Teddy grows silent at meals. His mom shoots looks at his pop. Teddy walks in the woods where he found Kate singing. He picks daisies. We see him closing his fist around the flowers. He opens his palm: yellow stains.

WE SEE HIM REACHING the brook now, across which is Beth's house, Beth hanging white sheets on her clothesline, the sun reflected off of the sheets like lighthouse beacons. He rushes down, trying not to think, to the water. Then he shuts his eyes and throws himself across the brook. On the other side, he breathes heavily, gripping his knees—he taps his fingers on his kneecaps, one-two-three-four.

When he looks up, Beth is still hanging laundry, her blond hair dropping straight down her back. He takes a deep breath, holds it, and heads toward her.

As he approaches, she turns to him teary-eyed; in her face is awareness and love.

"Oh, Ted." She holds a white bedsheet in her hands. Hers and George's. He stares, and she looks down and tosses the sheet over the line.

He continues toward her. We see her readying herself, expecting him. He pulls something out of his pocket. Her Dear John letter. He opens her hand and slides the letter between her fingers. She seems to weigh it, her stare going from it to him and back. We can tell she knows what it is without reading it.

He looks at the laundry line, the brook, the lawn. "Didn't know why I was keeping that until I seen you just now, I reckon." His face seems pulled back to an invisible point behind his eyes. "I buried that letter but it just kept coming back to me. I couldn't get rid of it."

She reaches out and holds him by the shoulders until he looks at her. "George is so bad, Ted. He doesn't love me." Her long eyelashes spike from her eyes.

She kisses him, throws her arms around him. He kisses her back. He almost gets lost in the kiss; then he stops, pulls away, backs off.

FINALLY, KATE'S HEALTH IMPROVES. We
see the doctor examining her: her eyes, her ears, her
mouth; she responds, able to respond, sweat wetting
her forehead. As the doctor slides his stethoscope under
her shirt, up over her chest, Teddy steps forward to
stop him.

"She'll be fine," the doctor says, misunderstanding.
"The fever should break in a day or two. Keep her out
of the water, though. I heard you saved her life."

"I reckon."

"The poor girl." The doctor repacks his tools and leaves
the room.

Teddy leans in and strokes the dark hair inked on the
pillow. "I'm sorry," he says.

He hears the doctor, in the hallway, ask his mom if it
was a suicide attempt.

LATER, WE WATCH HIM carry a bowl of water
and a towel into the bedroom, place the bowl on the
nightstand. He looks down at Kate as she sleeps. An
eyelash hovers, and he blows it off her cheek. He wets
the towel, wrings out the extra water, folds it up and
lays it on her forehead. He holds her hand and stares at
the two rings, tracing over her veins with his finger.

Something, a shadow, appears in the window, about forty feet away. Beth walking out of the woods he's walked through many times in these past days. She holds her skirt above her calves and gazes in at him.

AFTER HALF A WEEK, Kate recovers enough to take her meals at the kitchen table. She looks fragile still, but her cheeks are pink again, her eyes bright. We see her drinking the cherry soda Teddy's mom brought, Teddy smiling uncontrollably. Fresh daisies in the middle of the table. Kate reaches out and twists a petal loose.

"My daddy been around here?" she asks.

"I reckon we hop in the Studebaker and get ourselves back to the motel."

"You listening to me?"

"You're alive again, Kate. You came on out of that hole you were in and you're alive. When Red went into the Hole, he never came out, but you did."

"I thought you said that Red feller died trying to escape."

He drums his fingers, picks up his sandwich. She studies him: his ears twitching, his cheeks still skull-like, his eyes on the table. He bites into the bread to give his mouth something else to do besides talk.

"My daddy been around here?"

He shakes his head. She asks him to drive her over to her house.

HER DADDY SITS in his usual place, the spittoon at his feet, a tin of tobacco on a tree stump close at hand. He doesn't get up to greet them. Kate tidies the porch a little and then asks why he didn't come to see her. She looks between the house and him.

Her daddy lets fly at the spittoon. "You got your hero to look after you." He opens his hand and Kate puts the tin in it.

"She just wanted to see you," Teddy says.

Her daddy stands. Teddy moves in front of her, and she tugs his arm.

"It was nice to see you, Daddy," she says.

They back off of the porch. "Nice to see you," Teddy says.

Her daddy sits back down in his rocking chair, spitting.

IN THE EVENING, Kate sits at Teddy's kitchen table again, expressionless, Teddy fidgeting behind her. Every few minutes, he goes to the sink and pours water into his glass, but he doesn't drink. "I remember the town used to be full of stories about your pop," he says, not looking at her. "My pop"—he glances around though his parents aren't home—"never liked me before I was a hero. I reckon all's we got is each other."

"You got your momma," she says.

"I done been through the war and changed. My momma don't understand that."

Her jaw clenches. Then she pushes the table with surprising force. "Don't say a word against your momma." We watch her stomping out the door like a child. Across the street, someone is watching, or it might be the wind blowing through an oak.

Teddy rushes after her as the sun sets behind the clouds, his shoulders twitching. He looks around for her. He cups his mouth as if to call out, but instead, he drops into the grass, holding his head, his eyes on the spot where someone stood or didn't stand.

We can see Kate around the corner, leaning against the house, breathing hard, the wind swishing through the old tree at the yard's edge. She thinks she sees someone, too—a low branch hangs over the grass, and she reaches up for it. She traces over where a rope, or a belt, would wrap around it, traces an imaginary line down to the side of her neck. As she looks up at the branch, her fist beside her neck, she screams.

We see Teddy running around the side of the house to find her with her hand to the side of her throat, staring up as if at a sniper. He sprints forward and tackles her. She silences. His body buzzes on top of hers. She reaches up, brings his mouth down to hers.

LATER, they sit on the front step, the kitchen light illuminating their backs. Before them, Cracker's Neck stretches dark and impenetrable. He sits with his hands together between his knees, leaning forward on his elbows. She reaches for his hand, and he tenses up before she pulls away and covers her face.

She says: "I got her Daddy's cowboy belt like she asked, and then she said, 'Go on inside,' and I don't know why I done either."

They stare out into the darkness.

"I reckon everyone I ever known either left or had to be left."

As she meets his gaze, wanting him to do something, he feels his head pulsing.

THE NEXT MORNING, they eat breakfast with his parents. Sausage and cheese grits, Teddy's favorite. His pop flips through the paper. His mom watches them hopefully.

"Ain't y'all going back on your honeymoon?"

Kate tries not to blush as Teddy smiles at her. She looks away.

"You see they wrote you up in the news again today, son?" his pop asks. "When I talk about you down at the mill, every one of them wishes you was their son."

"Let me see that," Kate says.

His pop hands over the paper proudly. She glances at Teddy. He doesn't stir—he knows she is going to tease him. "I reckoned they'd get tired of you by now," she says. "They interviewed George Watson." He makes an effort. "They ain't got no one else left to ask but your wife."

We watch Teddy's mom at the mailbox as the Studebaker pulls away. She takes the mail into the kitchen and Teddy's pop asks if they're more fan letters. One envelope, Japanese stamps, no return address, she opens immediately—*Teddy, Army's on a witch hunt. Get a lawyer.* It's as if she already knew. She stuffs

the letter back in its envelope, opens the others in front
of her husband, for show, then pretends to drop them
all into the trash as she pockets the one from Japan.

TEDDY AND KATE HIKE the mile-long trail through
Natural Tunnel State Park, toward the eight-hundred-fifty-
foot channel, carved by glaciers through a limestone
ridge, at the end. The brush grows over the markers
as if to erase the path Daniel Boone first made. Teddy
walks carefully, watching Kate lead. A slight breeze
presses her clothes against her body. He stumbles.

"I reckon you can take off that engagement ring now,"
he says.

"I like it," she says, looking back at him. Something
about him seems a little off, but she twists the ring
and laughs. "It's the first one I ever got."

When they reach the tunnel, train tracks leading to
the other side, he shifts his weight and stares at where
they've ended up, as if their journey could have led
elsewhere. She takes his hand. "It's just a tunnel. I want
to see it." She pulls him along. His fingers flick into his
pocket, but nothing is there. He hears voices—maybe
his own. Eleven, ten, nine, eight. His eyes search the dark.

"Do you hear that?" he asks.

"You trying to scare me?" She pulls him again. Yet when she turns, at last, his face is pale and sweating. His mouth moves silently. His fingers slip out of hers. The voices in his head are a low, persistent rumbling.

"I ain't going in there."

"You said you wanted to come," she says.

"You said it was either here or Ball's Bluff. I can't go to them battlefields. I meant to give you the day you wanted."

She watches his left leg tremble, as if on its own.

She sighs; then she says, "Tell me why you can't go into that tunnel then."

He backs away.

"You told me before about your friend, Red. You told me you thought about me. Those were lies, weren't they?"

"They ain't lies." He presses his hand to his forehead and gasps. The voices grow louder—we can hear them, they're his own: *What's the hole?* he's asking. He speaks over them, shaking his head.

He starts to hyperventilate. Finally, she doubles back to him. She doesn't know what is going on, but she takes his arm, struggling to move him, to turn him away from the tunnel. They go a few steps, and then a few more, and the farther away, the calmer he becomes. They lurch about twenty feet before they stop and he leans into her; the voices disappear. She stands behind him, wrapping her arms tightly around his chest, resting her cheek on his back. We see her fear, her pity, her compassion.

Eyes squeezed shut, he says: "I didn't know if I was alive or dead. I did some things just to get back here. To get back here to you."

As he drives them to the motel, she holds his right hand between hers, twittering her fingers over his palm like a bird over a lake.

WE SEE THEM on a bright, windless day now, coming out of the drugstore, Kate holding a bag of root beer candies and teasing him as usual, asking if he remembers teaching her how to fish, once, in Claytor Lake, before his friends arrived; she says he always could be nice if he wanted to, or if no one else was around. What he wants now is to brush his thumbs across her freckles, but all he does is smile. Then, straight ahead of them, is Beth. She turns to him, in the middle of the sidewalk, and all of Virginia seems to shrink into a small dark space.

This time, he's on his back, legs bent in front of him. He opens his mouth to scream, or to murmur in defeat, but then Beth appears in the Hole, her body sliding over his. She moves up to his lips, and what light is left disappears.

He can smell the vomit again. His throat itches for a glass of water.

WE SEE KATE AND BETH taking him back to his house. Beth remains in the kitchen as Kate tends to him. She sits at the oak table, rubbing at her nails, looking for something to occupy her. She gets up to wash the dishes in the sink.

When Kate enters, Beth seems to be making herself at home.

"What's wrong with him?" Kate asks accusingly.

Beth continues washing.

"You hear me?" Kate says.

"I don't know."

"Then why'd you come along?"

Beth pulls a towel from the stove handle and dries a plate. Finally, she looks up, crying.

"We were engaged," Beth says.

"I know what you was."

Beth's hands drip onto the floor. "I reckon you know my husband, too. How he's like your daddy."

"Don't talk about my daddy," Kate says. She slams a cabinet door shut, looking in at the clean dishes Beth has stacked up. "I reckon your husband won't be happy to hear you been over here."

IN THE OTHER ROOM, we see Teddy coming to. He lies still, listening to the fight, staring up at the ceiling, past it, far away. His cheeks look sunken, his ears floppier. He tries not to hear. The day he was captured, a guard went down the line with a revolver, waiting for a prisoner to say something.

"You was here the other night, too, wasn't you?"

"You don't deserve him."

The bedroom shrinks, the girls' voices fade into the background.

We see him running out of the room, through the hall, the foyer, out the opened door no one thought to close, collapsing in the yard, shaking. When he wakes again, Kate and Beth stand over him, their argument abandoned.

"What's wrong?" Kate says. "What's happening to you?"

He looks between them, rubbing his forehead. "I love you," he whispers.

They can't tell whom he means.

"I love you, too," Beth says.

Kate sits beside him and picks handfuls of grass, dropping them in the yard. She watches her hands pick and drop as if they are someone else's. She pulls a hair off of her blouse, letting the breeze take it away.

When his mom runs up, she has them move him back into the house.

In the kitchen, Beth yanks at Kate's hand and pulls her around by it, as they try to keep their voices low. Teddy's mom is with him in the bedroom. When Kate pulls free, Beth bends over to catch her breath, her blond hair falling around her face.

"That's my ring," Beth says, panting.

"What are you talking about?"

"I reckon Teddy gave you my ring."

We watch Kate's face open in recognition, then close just as quickly, her blue eyes narrowing. She brushes her hair out of her face. "It ain't yours no more. I reckon you better leave before I call George Watson."

Beth breathes hard, then straightens up, trying to act dignified.

Inside the bedroom, we see Teddy's mom waving one arm around, brushing her eyes, her nose. Her other hand stays in her skirt pocket, closed over the letter from Japan.

AN HOUR LATER, Teddy drives back to the motel, gripping the wheel tightly, the countryside flying by the windows. Blue hills and dark green pines the same as Korea.

"I don't reckon you should be driving," Kate says.

He presses the accelerator.

"Hey, I'm talking to you."

He keeps ignoring her, but with a growing glimmer of fear.

"Theodore Dickerson, you ain't got no right. You done gave me her ring, and now you're trying to kill me?"

His foot slips, his eyes big and empty and lost.

LATER, HE TRIES TO TALK but she stares out the window, pinch-mouthed. When they pull into the motel lot, she hops out of the Studebaker and slams the door.

"I was never trying to hurt you," he says.

She stomps toward their room, though she has to wait for him to open it.

As the sun sets, they sit on opposite corners of the bed. He looks toward her. She looks away. The slanting light shines into the room, past her, into his eyes.

"Why'd you do it?" she asks.

"I reckoned I already had the ring. We was getting married so soon after."

She takes off Beth's ring and flings it against the wall; then she stares down at the wedding band. "No, Teddy. I mean, why'd you marry me? Don't you love Beth?"

He starts toward the ring, restrains himself.

"I can feel the bed shift when you move."

Finally, he says, "Before the war, everything seemed right. Now there's something wrong with me the Reds must have done."

"That's why you married me?" she says. "Because something's wrong with you?"

"I mean I got through that, Kate, and I found you." He rolls the hem of his shirt like a cigarette. "I reckoned you was the end of a dark time. I reckoned you understood me."

She tries to see him in her peripherals without turning back to him. "I know you changed," she says, "but sometimes I reckon it's this much"—she holds her hands apart—"and it's always more."

They shift their bodies, first he moves, then she does, until she blocks the sun and he can see her face—some emotion between touched and pained. Her shadow falls across his eyes, the sun glowing in her dark hair.

WE SEE HIM WAKING IN THE WOODS behind Beth's house, the letter from Japan in his pocket. He hears Kate calling. Ahead is the glint of a river. He listens, looks around him. For an instant everything seems beautiful, open, full of choices—until something draws him back to the water.

He hears Kate's shouts in the background, yet he rushes forward. Bodies bob in the current, reaching out to be rescued: first nameless POWs, one with a slice of metal where an eye should be, one with a hole in his side, then the cook stabbed in the neck, then Red. As he

approaches, an image of Kate appears, diving into the
bodies. He follows her, calling. Hands drag him down
inside the river. He hears Kate again, outside, but he
can't get to her. It's like if an egg is too strong and the
chick gets stuck inside, its skeleton molding to the shell.

HE WAKES UP IN BETH AND GEORGE'S BED,
their striped wallpaper around him, their antique
lamp on the nightstand beside him, their armchair in
the corner, their four-pane windows on the back wall,
parallel to their bed. Beth hovers over him, her lips
painted and full. "You went into the river. I saved you."

"You saved me?" He tries to remember.

"You were so darn hard to move," she says. She tugs on
his ear. He remembers she used to tug on his ear like that.

 "I saw Kate going into the water."

"There was no one," Beth says. "No one but you and me."

He eyes her mistrustfully. "You left me with no one,"
he says.

He perks up, hearing something at the window. "Kate."

Beth moves quickly, drawing the curtain, the fabric
blocking out most of the light. "Beth?" Kate calls. "The
door's open. I'm coming in."

We see Kate enter, out of breath, as Beth steps into the hall, closing off the bedroom behind her. "He ran off again," Kate says. "I saw your house. I thought you might could—" She lowers her head.

Then the lamp clicks on, light visible under the door. Kate pushes Beth aside.

"I've been in bed with him," Beth says. "He kissed me."

"I had to get to you, Kate," Teddy says. "I saw everyone I wanted to save in the river."

TEDDY AND KATE MAKE THEIR WAY back to the motel room. They don't turn on the lights. A rush to their movements, need. They pull each other through the door. We see their bodies approach, his hands asking, hers answering. We see them kiss, move together hesitantly, then less hesitantly.

Afterward, she turns on the lights, wrapped in the sheets that hang down from the bed and stretch across the floor to her body. He lies happily in bed.

She wants to know what haunts him. "I reckon you need help. Something bad is in you."

He tries to hold onto his happiness.

"Teddy."

"I done some things you can't tell your wife," he says at last.

"I reckon you done some things you got to tell your wife."

He looks away from her, thinking he can hear voices.

"Where do you go? When your eyes disappear. You go somewhere. Let me go with you." She tugs the sheets up around her again. Her white arms shimmer.

She says: "Sometimes I dream about my momma, clear as day."

"You want to go to her?" He turns back; she's catching his attention.

"I reckon she'd like you. You save folks."

He wrinkles his eyebrows and frowns. Her legs make a slender impression beneath the sheets. "It ain't your fault," he says. He shifts higher in the bed. "I want to get away, but the war is always out there."

He says: "I ain't a hero like they said. I'm just trying not to hurt so much."

She lies beside him now.

"After we tried to escape they took us back and beat us. They put me in the Hole."

"Where Red died?"

"I could smell him. I reckoned I could smell his smell different from the other dead. Then when I got out of the Hole I did anything they wanted. I wrote letters. I talked like I believed it. I stayed alive. But soon I started having these fits."

She turns onto her side, toward him.

"Kate?" He holds his breath.

"Someone had to take the fall. You saved them other boys from taking it."

He eyes his clothes on the floor, the letter from Japan poking out from his pocket. "Most of them other boys ended up dead."

IMAGINE THEM ON THE BEACH. Imagine a hazy afternoon too cold for swimming. Imagine her burying him in the sand, them knowing each other. She piles the sand on his legs, on his stomach, on his chest. When it reaches his neck, he pales, his eyes full of desperation. She understands. She holds his cheeks in her hands. Gradually, she brings him back.

A WEEK AFTER THEIR HONEYMOON, they're back in Teddy's house, lying on his bed. She lets her feet drop to the floor, lets him trace a finger over her leg. She pulls a bathrobe around her shoulders, flips her hair over the collar, and smiles. As he watches her slip out into the hall and down to the bathroom for a shower, a car door slams outside.

We follow his mom to the front door. Two soldiers step up in dress uniforms. She stands in the entrance, blocking their way, already scared and protective. When they ask for Corporal Theodore Dickerson, she feels as if they mean someone else.

Teddy sticks his head out of the bedroom. Kate pokes back out of the bathroom in her robe. "Go inside," he says, pleading.

"Corporal Theodore Dickerson," the first soldier says, "you're under arrest by the United States of America."

THEY TAKE HIM to the Fort Belvoir military prison. The first night, he has a seizure. The light disappears into Kate's freckles. Brown dots the size of months. Two days later, his mom and Kate arrive with a lawyer, a young kid eager to make an impression.

"They tried a major in a similar case not long ago. He only got a year, even with McCarthy after him. I could get you near that, but you have to tell me exactly what you did for the Reds."

Teddy stays silent, trying to read his mom and Kate. He doesn't want them to be afraid for him—or of him. They wait. He sees Kate losing her patience, uncomfortable, unsteady. Her cheek twitches as if hiding a nut inside.

"They say you gave the Reds information, that you signed a petition, recorded a speech." The lawyer licks his fingers and flips through his stack of papers. "That you led discussion groups 'alleging the United States was an illegal aggressor in the Korean Conflict and Communism should be embraced by POWs.' They say you already admitted to what you did."

Teddy doesn't react.

"It wasn't his fault," Kate says.

"Were you tortured?"

We see them expecting him to say yes—yet when he goes to answer, something in him refuses. He doesn't want to show how hurt he is. He doesn't want to say the Reds could make him do anything they wanted. He doesn't want to explain why others resisted when he did not. O'Neil—he can't explain this.

"Tell him, Teddy," his mom says. "Tell him you was tortured."

"Where's Pop?"

"I know you're getting moved to the medical ward tomorrow," the lawyer says.

"You don't know anything."

We see Kate's nervousness, her eyes darting, not knowing who or what to believe anymore. Teddy has lied before—their time together seems now as short as it was.

"If you were tortured, we have a case. We can use the trauma. We can use what happens to you here. Mental instability. It means you weren't in the right mind."

"I know what it is." His foot scrapes across the floor.

"Didn't the Army say he was a hero?" Kate says finally. "Didn't the papers?"

The lawyer waits.

"YOU MEAN HE'S CRAZY," she says. She looks away from Teddy. She flattens a crease in her skirt. She is thinking about her mother, about the bodies Teddy saw in the brook.

"I wasn't myself when I done them things. It means they changed who I was."

She brushes a hair from her cheek. "You're innocent—if you're innocent, you'll win."

A guard comes in and says it's time to go. The lawyer asks Teddy to think about it.

"It's only been two months," Kate whispers.

The guard leads him away. But as they reach the door, she rushes forward. She flings her arms around Teddy and kisses him.

"My daddy don't want me coming here no more," she says lightly, as they part. Her eyes leave two wet spots on his shirt, as if she is looking out from his insides.

As the guard pulls him behind the glass, she watches Teddy's mouth move—"I got to try this plea"—yet she can't hear him.

HE DREAMS they are back at Claytor Lake, but their positions switched, he at the edge, she with the woods behind her. "Crazy's crazy," she says. He looks over his shoulder at the water below. It recedes, ebbing away faster and faster, a hundred feet away, more, more. When he turns back to her, she's gone.

He dreams this again and again.

OUTSIDE THE MEDICAL WARD, Army engineers-in-training test dynamite. Teddy opens his eyes to a narrow space, a steel frame above, the explosions reverberating in the background. Light on four sides. Approaching feet.

He's under his bed. A nurse slides the bed away and he blinks into the room. She says he has a visitor. We can tell she knows what to expect, as she watches him.

In the ward, patients stumble by, a few nurses beside the worst cases, guards at the door, steel beds along the sides. He dusts himself off, checks his pockets (nothing) and turns to her. "What's that sound?"

"Told you last time. Not a war." She takes his arm. She leads him past a World War II poster on the wall— *Come hell or high water, cupid marches on*—walking slowly, making sure he doesn't disappear. In one corner, a man does the crawl stroke across the floor.

Teddy's parents wait in the cafeteria, soldiers guarding the door, the explosions going on outside. He sits across the table from them. His mom reaches for his hand. "You don't have a choice, Teddy. Please."

His pop looks dragged along, miserable at the thought of his son as a traitor.

"Frank," she says.

"What's all that damn sound?"

"Two weeks you ain't seen him."

His pop shifts, scratches the top of his ear. "Try the plea."

"I'll lose her," Teddy says. He leans forward. "I'll lose her."

We see his pop's relief, his mom crying. "Tell your momma you're a hero."

Teddy's eyes go blank. He grips the table.

When he's sentenced to ten years imprisonment and a dishonorable discharge, his mom sobs, Kate's daddy leaves the courtroom immediately. He tries to drag Kate with him, but she shakes him off. The bailiff appears at Teddy's side. His lawyer promises an appeal. Soon Teddy and the bailiff are alone with his parents and Kate in an empty room.

Teddy tries to aim their walk toward his wife, but his mom intercepts them. She falls upon her son, crying, so that he has to hold her up. His pop turns away.

"Ma'am," the bailiff says. He hesitates, then pries her off.

Teddy keeps his stare on Kate, even as his pop steps out and his mom struggles. We can hear Kate's daddy yelling from the hall. She stays. Her lips move. She doesn't break eye contact. He carefully deciphers her whispers: Soon as I can.

We know her thoughts are deep in the last months, trying to make sense of what's happened.

In Fort Belvoir, Teddy loses weight, refuses food, loses more weight. He sits on his bed, writes Kate a letter when she never arrives.

Dear Kate,

I reckon with all the big things happening, I forgot to ask about the small ones. Do you like movies? Do you like movie stars? I remember a picture I seen when I was younger, Random Harvest. Do you know that one? The feller gets hit by a taxi and doesn't remember a thing. He forgets his first love, his whole life—everything disappears. But the woman goes after him. They get married in his new life. He's a politician. They say it's good politics. They get caught in this relationship. You reckon maybe it's all for the worse. But then, at the end of the picture, he recognizes her. He knows her. He realizes that what he's got now is the thing he's always wanted.

WE SEE HIM SEIZING in the night, the few night nurses' silhouettes converging on his bed. They hold him down, stick a piece of wood in his mouth. His body lifts into the air, shakes, flails. He kicks one of the nurses in the arm. Finally, they get him under control.

We see him watching the engineers-in-training turning things to rubble, to start a new hospital and a nuclear plant, both to open in 1957. Kate still hasn't arrived. He won't eat. His face thins. He watches the guy in the corner try to swim across the tile.

It is winter again. He sees a dirt floor, men folded into each other, in his dreams. He sees stitches, smells gizzards.

After three weeks, the nurse leads a major through the ward to Teddy's bed, an older man with a limp, immediately trustworthy, who says he'd like to represent Teddy's appeal. Though he gets no reaction, he waves the nurse away. Teddy stares at the ceiling. The major pulls a chair over to the bed. "Your lawyer made several mistakes, Corporal. I've been doing this for over fifteen years. I know a few things. I know you were made a scapegoat and to let you off would have pissed off the higher-ups. I know they promised you immunity."

The major waits for Teddy to answer.

"You did no worse than Colonel Schwable, reinstated, or General Dean, Medal of Honor. Damn it, son. I've got letters from hundreds of people pledging their support."

Teddy reaches into his pocket, remembering his letter to Kate; he holds it to his chest as if blessing it, and then hands it to the major. "For my wife. Reckon you could get it to her?"

LATER, WE SEE TEDDY sitting with his nurse, getting his blood pressure checked, his angles sharp, bones that could put out an eye. Those floppy ears. He can play piano on his ribs again, the notes reverberating inside of him.

"I guess there's going to be an appeal?"

"I reckon," he says.

"You don't know?" The nurse listens to his heart. We see her awkwardness. "You have a girl, a wife. She hasn't visited?"

For a second, he thinks maybe she knows something. Then, ashamed of his hope, he tells her to leave him alone.

"Sorry," the nurse says.

In the corner, the man forever swims the crawl stroke.

We see the nurse trying again, Teddy's teeth grinding. "You know why he swims? He thinks he's a long-distance swimmer. He thinks he can break a record."

Finally, she gets her stuff ready to go. Teddy looks toward the entrance as if someone has entered the ward. "Could be plenty of reasons keeping her away. Her daddy. I reckon everything she thought I was got taken away from her."

MORE TIME PASSES. We see another nurse now, approaching a cleaned-up Teddy—getting over or giving up—standing near a group of patients talking about their withering health. At least he is away from his bed. At least he is eating again. She has checked his chart; he looks better than it says. We hear her clear her throat, not to sneak up on him.

"You have a visitor," she says. He hurries forward.

His pop waits in the cafeteria. Teddy slumps into the seat across from him. "What are you doing here?" he says. "You heard I ain't who you wanted me to be."

We can see his pop struggling to talk to his son, walking around the plastic chairs, unable to keep still, Teddy trying to remain angry but always wanting to please his father.

"Son," his pop says. "My son."

"Pop, if you asked me to bring you a belt to hurt me with, I reckon I'd bring it to you."

His pop steps forward, steps back, cries. He doesn't know how to ask for forgiveness. We can see Teddy having trouble registering where he is, hear him speaking as if Kate is there in the room with him, speaking back. He taps the table.

"I reckon everyone I ever known either left or had to be left."

"I should have loved you better," his pop says, misunderstanding. He hugs his son hard. Teddy lets himself be hugged.

AROUND SUNSET NOW, Teddy stares through the ward, concentrating. We see his tears: for his pop, for Kate, for everything gone wrong. He keeps concentrating, looking at the door of the ward, looking through bodies. He starts to seize. He can hear Kate's voice singing about old times not forgotten, about Dixie, echoing and hollow. He climbs down from his bed, dead-eyed, and gets under it. His concentration is not on his physical actions, not on his body. He is reaching into darkness. As the ward goes black, a white beacon appears in the middle of the floor, twirling.

He looks out from under his bed—and then she's there, a white dress hanging to her ankles, freckles all over, like she's a jigsaw puzzle of brown and white. She's chewing something: root beer candies. Her jaw is working. Pain flashes through his forehead.

She says something he can't understand, an explosion sounding outside. She mumbles. Water laps behind her eyes. He wants to say something that will make her stay. He wants to know what that is. He wants her to rescue him, carry him back to the Studebaker and drive across Virginia. Hold up her hands and measure how much he's changed this time.

For an instant, she looks at him as if he could convince her. A ring shines on her finger. He knows at some point, in their honeymoon, he convinced her, then lost her. But she could bring him back, put her hands on him and bring back that piece of him she thought he was. Whatever he was with her.

He tries to crawl forward to where she stands in a haze of daisies. His fingers tap tap tap tap. She sings faintly, look away. He concentrates, continues to seize, continues to try to cut through what is real and unreal, to what is alterable.

ACKNOWLEDGEMENTS

Thank you to Deena Drewis, editor extraordinaire;
to Phong Nguyen, Matthew Eck, and Kevin Prufer
for publishing a shorter, much different version of
this story in Pleiades; to Laura van den Berg, Kirstin
Chen, James Scott, Chip Cheek, Margot Livesey, and
others for their generous advice and friendship; to my
agent, Terra Chalberg; to the Howard Gotlieb Archival
Research Center at Boston University, where I did the
research that led to this story; to Chris Keene, who
helped shape the book when it was still a screenplay;
to Paul Yoon, James Franco, and all who showed their
support; and most of all, to my family, my well of narrative.